NIGHT LIFE

The Night Trilogy: Book Two

by

B.K. Bass

Published in the U.S. by B.K. Bass, 2021
Second Edition

ISBN: 9798516711695 (Paperback)
Second Edition, 2021

Published by B.K. Bass in the United States of America

First published by Kyanite Publishing, 2020

Cover art licensed from Dreamstime.com
Interior art used under Creative Commons license

B.K. Bass can be reached at https://bkbass.com/contact/

For behind-the-scenes access and the latest news, subscribe to B.K.'s newsletter here: http://eepurl.com/dpaU6f

Visit the author's website at https://bkbass.com

Books by B.K. Bass

The Ravencrest Chronicles

Seahaven
The Hunter's Apprentice
The Giant and the Fishes
Tales from the Lusty Mermaid, a Ravencrest Chronicles Anthology
The Ravencrest Chronicles: Omnibus One
Curse of the Pirate King (The Pirate King Duology: Book One)
Shadow of the Pirate King (The Pirate King Duology: Book Two)

The Night Trilogy

Night Shift
Night Life
Night Shadow

The Tales of Durgan Stoutheart

Warriors of Understone
Companions of the Stone Road (forthcoming)

The Burning Sands

Blood of the Desert
Into the Red Wastes (forthcoming)

Beyond the Veil

Parting the Veil

Standalone Novels

What Once Was Home

I opened my eyes to the dirty orange glow of sunlight diffusing through the shroud of smog covering New Angeles. Every part of my body hurt, and I wasn't sure how much was from being roughed up by the Russian mob or from sleeping it off in the alley. I rolled over on the cardboard box that had been my mattress. The homeless man who also slept here last night was already awake. The disheveled figure ran his fingers through a long beard, examined what he excavated from the tangled weave, and apparently decided that some finds were edible.

Suppressing my revulsion at the sight, I struggled to my feet. My tan suit and white shirt were stained with everything from desert dust to sewage filth and blood. The last two days were a roller-coaster ride, and yesterday especially had been a nightmare. After showing up at a routine crime scene in the wee hours of Wednesday morning, my partner and I discovered we had a Jane Doe on our hands. This was rare since everyone had an identification bar code tattooed on their wrist. But someone sliced hers off.

After a meeting with our not-so-inspiring leader at the police station—Captain Halsing—he gave us a three-day ultimatum to track down not only the perp on Jane Doe's murder, but also the supplier for Kristoff Tomlinson's drug habit. Kristoff was the mayor's son, and after he got into some trouble with the law, she wanted to cut off his supply at the top.

I leaned back against the brick walls lining the alley and rubbed the bridge of my nose as my brain worked on remembering how all the dots connected. The real twist of the knife was my primary lead, a titanium paint chip found at the crime scene. This high-cost automotive paint was used in bulletproofing limos and the such. Because of this, my suspect for the murder ended up being the mayor herself or her brother—one business mogul by the name of James Talbot.

It turned out Talbot was making regular payments to a flesh bar in Berdino called Dreamworks, where I suspected his nephew might have been a regular guest. The establishment was missing an employee named Evie Simms, one of their mainframe jack-ins. Our Jane Doe had a cyberjack in the back of her skull, and it became obvious she was our victim when I showed up at Evie's apartment to find it tossed and bloody. It was there I ran into a professional cleaner sent by the notorious Fixer Vic.

So yesterday, Frank and I went out to have a chat with Vic. We found out an enforcer for the Russian mob named Boris hired Vic to arrange the cleaning. And Boris was not the sort you say no to when he asks a favor. Evie wasn't somebody you'd expect to be the victim of a mob cover-up, so the payments from Talbot had to have something to do with it. Many suspected Talbot had ties to the Russian mob, but so did Kristoff, the former as a business partner and the latter as a customer of their drug trade.

Evie must have gotten mixed up in all of this somehow, and someone took her out of the equation. Figuring the mayor's son was in the middle of it all, Frank and I headed to a hospital where Kristoff was lying low to make sure the mob didn't decide to eliminate another variable.

I patted the pockets of my coat, searching for my smokes. Some sort of divine influence must have been looking out for me, because I found a crumpled pack with a half-dozen mangled—yet unbroken—cigarettes inside. My badge was still on me as well, although my sidearm was missing. I pulled out a cigarette, along with a lighter I had tucked inside the pack, and took a deep draw as I lit it up. I held my breath for a moment with my head leaned up against the cold bricks, then released a cloud of tension along with the contents of my lungs. I shambled weakly down the alley towards the main street and noticed one of the larger-than-life holovids on the side of a building was lighting up with the morning news.

As I gazed up at the broadcast, I couldn't believe what the news anchor was saying. "According to New Angeles Police Department officials, Kristoff Tomlinson—the mayor's son—is dead. He was abducted from his hospital room at St. Mary's Hospital late yesterday, where he was recovering from injuries inflicted by homicide detective Harold Jacobson last week. Hospital staff say Jacobson was seen removing Kristoff from the premises at gunpoint. Detective Jacobson has a history of police brutality, but it is unclear what his motive for assaulting and later abducting the mayor's son was."

Well, they got it half right at least. I *had* given the young man a thrashing, but when a hyped-up addict resists arrest, that's typically what's going to happen. They missed the part where Boris and his cronies had come along and abducted the both of us, along with my partner Frank.

The news anchor continued. "According to an eye-witness statement given by a local vagrant, Jacobson took Kristoff to a utility maintenance facility in the sewers beneath the city. There, his long-time partner—Frank Jones—confronted him. The witness reports that Detective Jones attempted to arrest Jacobson, but in the ensuing argument, the rogue officer shot and killed him. Kristoff Tomlinson attempted to escape during the scuffle, but Jacobson pursued and gunned him down in cold blood. Investigators say the cause of death was four gunshot wounds to the back, corroborating this claim."

"Shit," I swore under my breath and looked around. The people on the street were drudging about as they always did, most of them with downcast eyes and likely more concerned with their own problems than what the news had to say. Still, plenty would see this; and once the media had found you guilty, there wasn't much anybody could do to change things. After the word spread, nobody would believe it had been Boris that had squeezed the trigger on both men after he tied me to a chair.

The news vid wasn't done. "Police officials report overwhelming evidence to support the eyewitness statement, including Detective Jacobson's fingerprints on the murder weapon—which was found nearby. He should be considered armed and dangerous. If seen, citizens are urged to avoid contact and report his whereabouts to authorities immediately."

Shit. They were even fabricating evidence. Somebody with their hands on the strings were pulling them hard to make me disappear. The weapon in question was still stashed behind some palettes next to where I slept in the alley. My weapon was still unaccounted for, so maybe that's what they found. Either way, I was without a sidearm, since there was no way I could walk around with a hot piece.

I ducked back into the alley, wishing I had a hat to pull down over my face. That same face was plastered on the skyline for the entire city to see, and surely there was a holovid projection of the story on every block from here to the outskirts. The sad part of it was that Evie's death hadn't made the news. Nobody in this city cared if a hooker or a flesh bar jack-in like Evie died; hell, there were a dozen of those cases every day. Even

Frank wouldn't have made the news if he hadn't been in that sewer tunnel with Kristoff.

I heard a shuffling sound and looked over my shoulder to see the homeless man I had shared the alley with the night before walking towards me. "Hey bud, can I get one of those smokes?" The man looked up at the holovid and then back to me. "Uh... never mind," he said as he spun about and headed back into the alley.

"Great," I muttered. I needed to lie low, but I had work to do. Now not only was my best lead in Evie's murder case dead, but I was being pinned as the perp in *his* murder. To top it all off, I was also wanted as a cop killer now, and my only backup was the vic. Nobody was going to believe my word against the smear campaign already running the holovids—which was probably orchestrated by the same people turning the gears on the Evie Simms cover-up—so I was going to have to clear my name. I only needed to figure out how Evie got mixed up in all this, what her connection to the now-deceased Kristoff was, how his uncle James Talbot tied to it, whether the mayor was involved, *and* find proof that the Bratva—the Russian mob—was running the show; all while being hunted down by the law myself.

I pulled the pack of cigarettes from my pocket and gave it a shake. *Five left*. I was going to need more smokes, and I was going to need a lot of coffee.

* * *

I pulled the hood of the threadbare brown jacket low over my face as I walked through the bustling crowds of the city sidewalk. I was right in the middle of downtown, and the Friday morning rush was in full swing. The swarm of humanity pressed in on me from all sides. Drab business suits walked shoulder to shoulder with garishly colored casual clothes. Conservative haircuts bobbed up and down next to mohawks and dreadlocks. The city was home to all kinds of cultures, and nowhere was this more apparent than in the bustling business district which laid in the center of it all.

Bits of discarded trash stuck to my bare feet as I made my way. One would have thought a nice suit would have been a fair trade for the homeless man's rags, but the old codger had driven a hard bargain and insisted on taking my shoes as well. He saw the news holovid and knew it was a seller's market, so I was forced to take the deal. Still, walking through the city barefoot was better than being arrested for a double homicide.

I would have loved nothing more than to head back to my apartment for some fresh clothes and to replace my lost sidearm, but it would have been swarming with cops by then. I needed to go underground, and fortunately I knew just the person to help me out.

Unfortunately, I would have to hoof it all the way to The Dale—a part of the city known as Glendale back before the big quake sent the coast of California sliding into the Pacific. The area was a hotbed of criminal activity even before the quake. After the region was rebuilt and became the megalopolis of New Angeles, The Dale quickly returned to its roots and was once again a haven for the criminal underground. Most likely this was because the area was planned as a ghetto from the outset and crammed full of tenements housing some of the poorest citizens of the city—many who were driven to crime in a desperate struggle for survival.

By mid-afternoon, the monolithic office and residential towers of downtown gave way to mid-size apartment buildings and scattered parks in Griffithsville, one of the few wealthy parts of the city. The neighborhood housed business tycoons who worked downtown but choose not to live in the towers. I stumbled into one of the parks—an expanse of green space compared to the rest of the city, but little more than a back-yard garden outside the sprawl—and plopped down on an iron bench along the flagstone path.

My feet were raw and bleeding, and my chest was pounding from the exertion of walking all morning. I pulled the cigarette pack out and peered inside. *Two left*. These probably weren't helping with my breathing problems, but today was not the day to decide suddenly to get healthy. I almost smoked another, but given the ground left to travel, I opted to ration them out and wait a while. Deciding on a brief rest in lieu of the scarce chemical stimulation, I laid down on the bench and shut my eyes for a few moments.

I must have fallen asleep, because it was nearly dark when I something hard striking my shoulder woke me. I rubbed the sleep from my eyes and held my hand up to block the blinding light somebody was shining in my face.

"You can't sleep here, dirtbag," a gravelly voice said.

The light moved aside, and the dull glow of the park's lamps lit a patrol officer standing over me with a flashlight in one hand and a baton in the other. My heart almost leaped from my chest and ran away as the morning's memories flooded back into my mind. I was a wanted man, a supposed cop-killer, and here was some hot-under-the-collar beat cop staring me down.

I ruffled my hair and pulled the hood of the jacket down as low as I could as I sat up. "Sorry, officer. Didn't mean to fall asleep."

"Looks like you're in the wrong part of town, too. You better get out of here before you get dragged in for vagrancy. What are you doing here, anyway?"

"Just passing through on my way to The Glen," I said as I stood. Pain shot through my feet as I put my weight on them, but I did my best to hide any reaction. Any good vagrant would be used to going bare-shod.

"Well, see you get there before you decide to take another nap. And for God's sake, man, find a bar of soap. You smell like a sewer." With that, the officer turned and walked back to the squad car perched on the side of the street. He climbed in, pulled the door down behind him, and drove off without another word.

I must have some luck left, I thought. I'd been more likely to be fleeced for anything of value and beaten than given a warning. And if he had recognized me, I would have been in store for a far worse fate. He was right, though. I needed to get out of Griffithsville before another beat cop with a less charitable demeanor came along.

I hustled out of the park and set into an even pace along the sidewalk before pulling out a smoke and lighting it up. The warmth felt good as it filled my lungs, and my still-racing heart calmed down as the nicotine went to work. I glanced at the barcode on my wrist after taking another drag. There was a pile of cash behind that simple tattoo. Not a big one, but enough for what I needed. But I knew the second I scanned it, every computer in every patrol car in the city would light up with my location. Before I could get more smokes, or get to work, I needed to get my money transferred to a clean account and replace my ink. Unfortunately, that was also going to cost me.

It was dark and the night had come alive by the time I shambled into The Dale. Boxy tenements rose all around, looking like clones of each other stamped along San Fernando Avenue. There were more people in the streets than there had been downtown, and I easily blended into the sea of desperation and filth. Pushers and prostitutes hawked their wares in the open, with little fear of the police showing up. Gangbangers patrolled the streets, armed with everything from iron pipes to assault rifles. This was their turf, and most cops knew better than to invade it without a squad of enforcement bots to back them up. Mountains of trash filled the back alleys, some of it predating the sanitation strike. Even the flies ignored the fact the sun had long since fled below the horizon, happily buzzing along with the neon lights.

The last time I'd been here, Frank and I had been chasing down a lead on a missing person; some corporate hotshot in the mayor's pocket. We knew somebody had the suit's barcode after his assets started getting withdrawn through several shell accounts and some nobody started spending like a high roller. We caught him with a bogus code freshly spliced onto his wrist, which had come from some other nobody that had gone missing. Frank and I paid a visit to a skin trader named Gregory, who specialized in making high-profile criminals disappear and redistributing access to high-value bank accounts. I had history with the man, having roughed him up a few times back when I was on the beat and before he came into favor with the Bratva. I was sure Gregory was the man to slice the suit's barcode, but we could find no proof—or any sign of the body, for that matter. Gregory was good, and that was why I found myself standing on his doorstep.

A burly guard in a dark suit stood before the nondescript basement door, something you'd miss behind the piles of trash if you weren't looking for it. He was a head taller than me and as broad-chested as a gorilla. He squinted as he looked me over, then his nose wrinkled and he took a step back. "You smell like shit," he said in a thick Russian accent.

"Yeah, I've been hearing that a lot today."

"Get lost before you end up in one of these bags," the Russian said as he waved the bull-pup rifle in his hands towards the piles of black plastic bags surrounding us.

"I need to see Gregory."

"And why would Gregory want to see you?"

I held up my wrist, exposing the barcode tattoo. "Either I see Gregory, or I go buy a coffee at the corner javamat and call every cop in New Angeles down on this block."

"And what makes you think you're so special?"

I groaned and shook my head as I felt around for my last smoke. "Don't you watch the news? They've only been plastering my face on every holovid between here and Berdino since sunrise." I watched realization dawn in his eyes as I lit the cigarette. I took a long drag and let the smoke waft out as I added, "And, there's money in the bank. I want to talk business."

The bruiser pressed a finger to a pin on his lapel and whispered something. A static-filled response came back a moment later, and he pushed the door open while saying, "Down the stairs, second door on the left."

I sidled past the guard, my feet leaving a trail of bloody footprints as I padded down the stairs and along the dimly lit corridor. Conduits and pipes accented concrete block walls, and ductwork that had more holes in it than the jacket I was wearing dominated the ceiling. I stopped at the second door and knocked.

"What are you waiting for, the butler? Get your ass in here," a gravelly voice shouted from the other side.

I pushed the door open and stepped inside as a rush of cold air stung my eyes. The room was larger than I expected, but still felt cramped from the low ceiling run through with pipes and ducts. The place was cold; not freezing, but chilly enough to be uncomfortable in the beggar's rags I was wearing. I had to stoop to make my way to the center of the room, where an array of tables covered in lab equipment, surgical tools, and metal boxes surrounded an old man who sat hunched over a small workspace. There was a metal tray on the table, and on it rested a disembodied forearm. Wrinkled and gnarled fingers make a deceptively deft cut with a scalpel, and the man pulled a perfect square of flesh away from the wrist. He placed it on a glass slide, poured some liquid over it, and sealed it with another piece of glass before depositing it into one of the metal boxes. Inside were row upon row of similar slides.

"One moment," he muttered as he stood with a groan, lifted the box, and walked to a row of freezers set along the back wall. Once he had deposited the grisly collection with a dozen similar cases, he turned back to me. "Well, I'll be damned. If it isn't Harold Jacobson, the most wanted man in New Angeles. I should have known you'd end up here."

"It's good to see you too, Gregory," I said as I rolled a metal stool over and took a seat opposite him at the table.

"Hmph," the old man grunted as he sat down. "Don't try that *old friend* bullshit on me. I work with the Russians now, remember? Everybody's an old friend with them until they decide you're not valuable and put a bullet in your head."

"Lots of that going around," I muttered, the memory of Frank's face coming apart flooding into my mind like an unwanted call from an ex-wife.

"Hmm? The way I hear it, you've taken after them. I don't buy it though. You're an asshole, but you're not a cop-killer."

"Thanks."

"Don't thank me yet." Gregory slid his chair to the side and grabbed a transparent tablet from another table before rolling back. He punched a few security codes in, then scrolled through some sort of database. "I hear you want to talk business, so let's cut the crap and get to it. You need a new tag; that's why you're here."

"You're as insightful as ever, old man. Are you sure I didn't just come hoping to buy a new pair of shoes?" I held up one of my cut and filthy feet.

Gregory grunted at the sight of it. "I can take care of that too, but it'll cost you."

"What's new?"

The old man nodded as he continued to scroll through the hundreds of entries on the tablet. "I'm guessing you want something incognito. Some good-for-nothing that nobody noticed was missing."

"Yeah, but it has to be clean," I said. The last thing I wanted was to trade down to a petty crook. Even that might get me too much attention. And with my face as public as it was, that was the last thing I needed.

"Don't insult me," Gregory said. "I don't sell tainted goods. You need the best, and that's why you came here."

As usual, the old man was full of himself. If I had wanted the best, I'd be in the back room of a surgical clinic downtown with a proper doctor who traded skin as a side gig. Instead, I was in some dirty, poorly lit basement with a washed-up mortician who lost his license when his personal fetishes led to one-too-many corpses being buried missing a foot.

Gregory sat me in what looked like an old dentist's chair and strapped my arm down. "You want something for the pain?" he asked.

"Let me guess," I muttered, "it'll cost me."

"Nothing's free."

"Yeah, but just a local." I didn't trust him enough to be put under. I'd probably wake up missing a kidney.

The old man spun around on the stool and rummaged in a rusty old toolbox. He retrieved a syringe that was thankfully wrapped in plastic, along with a scalpel and a pair of forceps.

"You sure those are clean?" I asked.

Gregory jerked a thumb back to the main work desk. “See the miniature autoclave? It’s not there for show. Giving people gangrene is bad for repeat business, after all.”

It was always about the bottom line with this guy, but at least I wouldn’t have to worry about losing my arm to an infection. Gregory opened the syringe and slid the needle into my arm without warning. The quick prick was nothing compared to the burning sensation of the anesthetic as he squeezed it into the flesh around my identification tattoo. He repeated the process two more times, again with the bedside manner of a retired mortician.

“Okie dokie...” Gregory tossed the empty syringe into a metal coffee can and rolled over to the freezers. He picked up the tablet and checked something on the screen before opening the door. He thumbed through one of the boxes, muttering. “Nine seven five forty-two. Nine seven five forty-two. Nine seven— Aha! Here we are.”

For a criminal barcode slicer working out of the basement of an abandoned tenement, Gregory was surprisingly organized.

He rolled back over with a glass slide in his hand and set it in a small dish of warm water, which let off ribbons of steam in the chilly room. He reached down and pinched my forearm, hard enough my skin turned red even though I couldn't feel anything. "Numb yet?"

I nodded.

"Good, time to get to work, then." Gregory tore open the plastic wrap containing the other implements and, with the scalpel in one hand and the forceps in the other, he sliced into my forearm. Compared to the gruff way he went about everything else; he handled the blade with a surgeon's precision. He cut slowly and steadily, the depth of the blade never wavering. He made four even lines with almost perfect right angles, then dabbed away the blood with some gauze.

"You might not want to watch this part. Most don't," he said.

"I'd rather know what you're up to."

"Good for you." The old man chuckled as he pinched the corner of the square with the forceps and pulled up, gingerly slicing under it with the scalpel. He pulled the skin higher as he went, carefully lifting the barcode away from my arm and cutting until it popped free. He then turned and dropped it into a nearby trash can.

"Not keeping that one?" I asked.

"I told you," he said as he dabbed away at more blood. "I don't sell hot codes, and that's one of the hottest this city has seen in a while."

I sighed as the weight of the moment hit me. This was just the first step in a long crusade. Seeing my face up on the holovids and knowing I was being framed for Frank and Kristoff's murders was one thing, but having my ID sliced made it feel real. My mind had been as numb all day as my arm was in that moment, and suddenly all the physical ailments washed away as the reality of my situation struck home.

"All done," Gregory said. I looked down in surprise. While my mind had been drifting off, the cutter had affixed the new barcode and cauterized the seams with a surgical laser.

He untied my arm and gave me a chance at a closer look. I twisted my wrist, flexing the newly affixed skin. It was swollen, but didn't seem altogether unnatural. The skin tone was too pale, but that would correct in time. "You *are* good."

"Tell me something I don't know." Gregory hobbled over to a locker on one wall, opened it up, and rummaged around. He tossed a pair of old work boots onto the floor, followed by some dirty blue jeans, a black button-down shirt, and a charcoal-gray trench coat. "Don't suppose you have a hat to match?" I asked.

Gregory glared at me with one eye half-closed, turned back to the locker, and came back with a navy-blue baseball cap with the New Angeles Rockets team logo on the front. Seeing my obvious frown of disapproval, he added, "You take what you can get."

Resigning myself to abandoning my usually dapper fashion sense, I stripped out of the beggar's clothes and put on what Gregory had offered. I didn't ask how much he was taking out of my account for them as his fingers worked furiously on the tablet. I didn't want to know, and there was nothing I could do about it.

"Okay, *my friend,*" Gregory said in a horrible impression of a Russian accent as he lit up a cigarette. "Your new name is Jasper Rogan. You were a sanitation worker who went missing after the strike started. No family—nobody to come looking for you or ask questions. A buddy of yours, one Gordon Hewitt, tried to file a missing person's report, but the NAPD was too busy to do the paperwork." The old slicer set his smoke in a glass ashtray and started to clean up around the old dentist's chair.

Sounded about right. A lot of trash men went missing around that time. Some just hit the bottle hard and ended up rolled over in an alley. Others were so deep in debt before the strike even started, they were desperate for a fresh start.

As I pulled the coat on, I turned to Gregory and asked, "Say, you haven't done any special jobs for the Russians lately, have you? Maybe something on the road?"

"Special? No, not that I can recall," Gregory answered as he placed the tray of bloody instruments into the microclave on his desk.

"You sure? No house calls? I saw a job recently that was exceptionally fine work; 'the best', as you described your own. A young girl with a cyberjack. Pretty thing with bright orange hair."

Gregory picked up his butt from the ashtray, took a quick puff, and stamped it out with a shaking hand.

"I don't do house calls." He stood and stepped around the desk, gesturing towards the door. "Now, you're going to want to put some ice on that to keep the swelling down. And don't try scanning it for about twelve hours. It needs time to settle into place. If you let it swell, it'll take longer."

I stood and walked toward the door. Gregory sighed as I passed by. He must have been relieved, thinking I was leaving without more questions. "One thing..." I muttered, turning back to the little man. "You haven't been to Monterey Park lately? Maybe Catawba Village?"

He was sweating, which was quite an accomplishment in the cold basement. The fog from his breath came in rapid puffs. "No, can't say I have."

As he reached out to open the door, I grabbed him by the wrist and gave it a quick twist. He yelped in pain as I jerked his arm behind his back, but I clapped my other hand over his mouth before it could grow into a full-on scream. As I led him back to the table, I said, "You know, for some reason, I don't believe you. I think you did this job and you don't want to talk about it."

He tried to say something, but with my hand over his mouth, it was too muffled to make out. I pulled up on his arm and down on his shoulder, sending his face crashing into the table next to the microclave. I popped the door open and grabbed the scalpel out of it. It was already hot enough to burn my hand, but I ignored the pain. Steam rose from the blade like smoke from a California wildfire as I held it just before Gregory's face. "Scream, and you lose an eye," I said as I pulled my hand away from his mouth.

"You're a cop. You can't do this," he whimpered.

I twisted the hand holding the scalpel, showing him his own handiwork in the form of the bootleg identification stamp newly cauterized onto my wrist. "Do I look like a cop to you? Now, tell me about Evie Simms. Who hired you to cut her ID, and where is it?"

"I don't know," he said as tears ran down his cheek and dropped onto the table.

"You don't know what? Who, or where?"

"Both. Neither. It was all handled over the dark net. I got an order, and I did the job. I never met anybody in person."

"What about the stamp?"

"There was a dead drop. I packed it in a cryo case and left it behind a dumpster."

"A dumpster where?"

"Behind the club."

"What club?"

"I'm not telling you anymore, they'll kill me."

"And you think I won't?" I ran the scalpel down Gregory's cheek to stress my point. "Don't scream," I reminded him.

The little man whimpered and whined like a kicked puppy, then caught his breath.

"What club?" I repeated.

"Dreamworks. They sent me to her apartment to cut her stamp. Then they told me to drop the cryo case off behind the dumpster in the alley behind Dreamworks, by the back door."

I let go of Gregory and put the scalpel down. *Sergei, you slick bastard.* The club owner acted surprised Evie didn't show up for her shift the other day, but he must have known all along why she wasn't there.

"Are you done?" Gregory asked.

"Yeah, except for one thing."

The old man grabbed a cloth from the table and pressed it over his bleeding face. “What’s that?”

“I need a gun.”

CHAPTER THREE

Gregory was generous with the gun, even throwing in plenty of ammo and an extra clip. It was a .45, bigger than I usually carried, but still smaller than Frank's old hand cannon. The whole thing was brushed steel and had the serial number filed off. It was probably a hot piece, but I was hoping just waving it around would be enough to get the job done. If I had to fire it, anything I was using would be hot at that point. I even got half a pack of cigarettes out of the deal. Gregory had protested about them, albeit briefly.

The bruiser by the door gave me a silent nod on the way out as I shoved the pistol into a shoulder holster Gregory had also thrown in as a gratuity for doing business with him. I instinctively went to tip my hat, then realized how ridiculous I probably looked as my fingers touched the brim of the baseball cap. Still, it would help hide my face from the cameras. I pulled it lower and squeezed the sides in tight, curling the brim so it hid my eyes as best as could be expected.

The old work boots clomped on the concrete sidewalk as I made my way down the street, crossed over, and headed east. It was a long trip from here to Berdino, and if I was going to pay Sergei a visit, I would need some wheels. I could take my chances on the barcode and try flagging a cab, but with my luck it wouldn't work. Also, my funds were limited and every dollar I spent needed to matter. No, I needed to find myself a new ride, so I turned down the ramp of a parking garage under one of the many apartment buildings lining the street.

As I walked through the garage, a few sports cars caught my eye. Flaming red and blazing yellow filled my vision for a moment, then I continued to peruse my options. Whatever I was in would be reported as stolen in the morning, so it needed to blend in. Even better if the owner didn't have enough money to bribe his claim to the top of the work queue. With luck, it would be a month or two before the report was even filed.

"Aha," I muttered as my eyes rested on the perfect ride. An old gas-burning sedan, which was probably cobalt blue ten years ago, sat rusting in one of the furthest spaces from the building's elevator. Not only could the owner not afford to maintain the car, he also couldn't afford a reserved parking space. The tires were nearly bald, but serviceable. A few flecks of blue paint still clung to the rust and gray primer that dominated most of the vehicle. The windows were intact, and either darkly tinted or very dirty. This was my new ride.

I pulled on the handle and the driver's side door popped open with a squeak. The owner probably wouldn't even care if it got stolen, granted they had another way to get around town. Given the amount of dust inside, they were already relying on the metro. Gas wasn't getting any cheaper, and taking the train was usually more cost-effective than burning fuel. Most people had electric cars these days, but finding an old smokemaker was a hell of a lot cheaper way to pick up some wheels—but when someone is that broke, they probably can't afford to keep it running.

Leaning in under the steering wheel, I popped the electrical panel off from under the dash, threw it in the back, and dug through the wiring harness inside. Finding what I was looking for, I yanked two wires free and twisted them together. I pulled a third loose and ran it across the exposed copper of the other two. Sparks jumped from the contact, and the engine roared to life. I gave it some gas to keep it running, shimmied up into the driver's seat, and pulled the door closed. I tested the wheel and found it locked in place, but a good jerk broke the steering lock and I was ready to go. As luck would have it—and at this point, I was surprised I had any luck left—the old car had nearly a full tank.

A rainbow of neon flashed by like the thoughts flowing through my mind as I drove down the road. Everything was pointing towards Sergei and Dreamworks. The victim, Evie Simms, was one of his employees. James Talbot, the mayor's brother, was making regular payments to the flesh bar through shell companies and was a known associate of several high-ranking Russian mobsters. A likely regular customer was Kristoff Tomlinson—the mayor's son and Talbot's nephew—and he was hunted down and killed by the Bratva enforcer Boris just days after Evie's murder. And now Gregory—who was also working for the Russians—had confessed to slicing her ID off and dumping it at the club. I didn't think Sergei was the mastermind pulling the strings, but if nothing else, he was a fly caught in the center of the web. What wasn't making sense was how Evie was mixed up in all of it.

The routine flash of angular neon and lettering faded as I approached Berdino, replaced with glowing adverts which were no less garish, but more refined in form. Purple, red, blue, green, and yellow all twisted into the forms of palm trees, cocktails, and dancing girls. The towering tenements of Can Town gave way to lower structures that had space between them for lawns and above-ground parking. Names like 'The Upper Room', 'Nightingales', and 'Amonar's Grotto' graced the face of progressively more ornate buildings with robust architectural elements like porte-cochères, columns, and marble facades.

Dreamworks sat on a corner lot like a diamond nestled atop a pile of gemstones. Bright green lettering spelled out the name of the place, bordered on either side by tasteful yet suggestive female forms wrought in purple neon. I didn't bother pulling up to the valet in the old beater. Better to find a shadowy spot in the alley behind the club. As I walked around to the front, the smooth notes of soft jazz were already filling my ears. It was a far cry from the thumping bass permeating most of the city; just another sign I was on the other side of the tracks.

The bouncer at the door, a brick house in a suit with a shaved head, held up a hand to stop me before I even got close. I pulled my badge out of the jeans and flashed it just quick enough for him to get a glint of bronze, but not long enough to read the name underneath. That was assuming he *could* read, but I wasn't taking any chances.

"Business or pleasure?" he asked, his gravelly voice devoid of patience as other, more appropriately attired patrons approached from the valet stand.

"Business," I said as I shoved the badge back in my pocket.

"Mister Zaetsyev isn't conducting official business tonight. You'll have to call for an appointment."

"He asked me to put fifty on his favorite horse," I said, holding my arm out and flashing my bar code. I tried to keep it in the shadows. The bruiser probably wouldn't care it was a fresh splice, but I couldn't afford to take any chances.

"Fifty, eh? He's usually more generous with his bets." The bouncer crossed his arms and planted himself squarely in front of the entrance.

Dammit. I knew I was low-balling the guy, but it couldn't hurt to try. "Did I say fifty? I meant a hundred."

"That sounds more like it." The big man pulled his phone out of his suit jacket, tapped a few times, then held it out. I checked the numbers on the screen to make sure he set it to pull a hundred dollars and not a penny more, then held my wrist under the screen. A blue glow lit my barcode, barely visible through the transparent pane of glass filled with the banking app's interface, and a dull chime signaled they completed the transaction. As the bouncer put the phone away, he added, "I hope the horse doesn't get out of line. Hate to see it *retired* early."

His meaning was as clear as the bribe had been. I nodded as he stood aside, then made my way into the club. I was looking for answers, not trouble, but the threat would not dissuade me from doing what I needed to get what I was after.

The front room looked as it had the other day: velvet couches lined with men in suits and women in much less. I refrained from taking a good look around, kept my head down, and headed straight for the door to the back rooms. The busty blond at the bar shouted something about having to register for a VR suite before heading back. Another bouncer took a step over with a hand held out to stop me, but a quick flash of the bronze shield was all it took to change his mind. I was confident everybody on the Dreamworks payroll was at least aware there was dirty laundry in the back, but not being bankrolled enough to get in my way if they were working the front. It was the goons behind the locked doors hiding Sergei's secrets I had to worry about.

The first of these doors was only twenty feet down the hall. Sergei's office, where Frank and I had met with the Russian club owner under the pretense of a code enforcement inspection. We chased a circumstantial pair of leads: our victim's cyberjack and the expensive paint chip next to the dumped body. Honestly, we were chasing a hunch more than a lead, but it paid off. We found out Evie Simms didn't show up for her shift that day at the club, and a later search of her apartment revealed the scene of the murder.

Now, the threads wound their way back here. Somebody took Evie's body to Monterey Park and dumped her naked in the rain while Gregory dumped the identification tattoo at Dreamworks. I still didn't know who was calling the shots, but the calls came through the desk behind these double doors.

They were locked. Probably the first of many doors I'd have to kick in before I found the truth behind Evie's murder, and the evidence I needed to clear my name. Hardened leather met heavy oak with a crash. Wood splintered around the aluminum lock, and bits of hardware clinked as it skidded across the marble floor. I strode into the center of the room and drew my pistol before the doors banged against the jams and swung back closed behind me. The rest of the hardware crashed to the floor as the doors drifted back open, their broken malaise a parody of so many souls losing themselves in the virtual reality suites down the hallway.

Sergei spun around in the chair behind his desk, his jaw hanging open wider than that of the red-haired strumpet whose head was in his lap. She jumped to her feet and let out a shriek of surprise, her bare breasts swaying back and forth as she tried to decide which way to run. I waved the gun to my left, and wiping her mouth with the back of her hand, she ran past and fled the office.

Sergei struggled to close his pants, all the suave demeanor once held in check by his tuxedo and bow tie now gone with his most personal of assets exposed. "What the hell? Who the fuck do you think—" Recognition dawned in his eyes and anger turned to shock, then melted away to be replaced by fear. "Harold Jacobson? You were already a dead man before tonight, but after this your fuse just got cut short."

The slick Russian reached under his desk, either going for a piece or a panic button, but I was sliding over the polished redwood before he found what he was looking for. Both feet took him square in the chest and sent him crashing to the ground. The floor-to-ceiling screens covering the wall behind him displayed a tropical beach complete with nude sunbathers, all casting a bright glow on the prone figure in the otherwise dark room.

I sat on the edge of the desk, the gun held casually in one hand as I fished out my smokes. "I need to talk to your girl."

"Then why did you wave her out?"

"Not that one. The one hooked up to your server."

"Impossible. She's working," Sergei said, waving his hand in dismissal as he sat up and tried to regain his composure.

"Then unplug her."

"I can't do that. If I unplug the system in the middle of operations, it'll render her, and everybody connected to her, catatonic. My nightclub would be a vegetable patch."

"There's got to be safeguards. Some sort of emergency exit protocol. Turn it off... Now." I jabbed the pistol towards him on the last word, just to make sure I got my point across. Shadows flitted across the wall as two figures entered the room behind me. "And tell your goons to head outside, unless you think they're faster than a bullet."

The shadows stopped. Sergei glared at me, silent while he considered his odds. He must have decided he wasn't a gambling man that night, because he waved the goons off. He climbed to his feet, smoothed out the rumpled tuxedo, and added, "But, you're just putting off the inevitable. They're going to come for you twice as hard after this."

I followed Sergei down the hall towards his server room with the gun leveled at the small of his back. All the time, I was hoping 'they' *would* come after me. At least then I could find out who they were and deal with them face-to-face instead of chasing shadows.

"You can still leave here alive. Just walk away, and I won't tell them you were here," Sergei said over his shoulder as he stood motionless before the security door to the club's server room.

I jabbed the barrel of the handgun into the small of his back. "Open it."

His fingers danced over controls on the wall and a small panel slid aside. He pressed his hand on a scanner and leaned forward. As the system scanned his handprint, another sensor analyzed his retinal pattern. There was a soft, pleasant chime, followed by a series of metallic clicks as the locks on the door released. He turned as if to invite me to go first, but I waved him forward with the pistol.

The Russian opened the door and stepped inside. Cool air rushed out as I followed him, and the hum of air rushing through a series of climate control vents filled my ears. Banks of computer equipment and a forest of monitors lined the room, and in the center was a massive virtual reality mainframe flanked by two reclining seats. Each held a shapely young woman.

"Which one do you want?" Sergei asked as he walked up to a terminal between the chairs.

I recognized the woman on the left from the other night when Frank and I paid Sergei our first visit. She had been working the same shift Evie had missed after her murder. I gestured towards her. "That one."

"I don't know what you hope to get from her," Sergei muttered as his fingers flew across the terminal's keyboard.

"Answers."

"Hmph." Keys clicked and a series of indicators on the terminal's monitor changed from green to red. Cries of outrage and groans of frustration flowed into the small space from the hallway behind us as the shutdown sequence ejected patrons from whatever high-cost sexual fantasies they had been engaged in. The woman twitched with each flash of red, her mind also being jerked from the simulations. From the screens above her station, I could tell she was servicing about a dozen clients at once through the virtual network. Each simulation was independent of the others, mostly run by the computer itself, but using the human brain connected to it to lend a genuine personality to each.

Sergei typed in a final set of commands and lights around the woman's head flashed yellow. She gasped as her mind was disconnected from the machine. Her eyes fluttered open, weakly at first. She blinked against the real-world light that she had probably not seen in hours. "What the hell, Sergei," she muttered, her voice slurring slightly as she struggled with the VR hangover. There was a whir of servos and a short, slender rod retracted from the back of her head. Cables connecting it to the mainframe wobbled as the mechanism pulled back and parked in a standby position. She sat up and rubbed the back of her skull as the cyberjack there, just like the one Evie had, closed a protective iris of shiny aluminum. She pulled her hair back and tied it into a low ponytail with an elastic which had been around her wrist, covering the cybernetic implant with practiced ease.

"Boss," a gruff voice called from the hallway. "There's a bunch of pissed off people out here."

Sergei waved him off. "Give them refunds, or free sims and drinks. Just shut them up or get rid of them."

"What's going on?" the woman asked.

"Magdela," Sergei said, "this man *insists* on talking to you." He punctuated the statement with a gesture towards the gun in my hand.

"Oh." Suddenly, her eyes grew large as she realized this was no regular interruption. "Oh, fuck." Fear filled them as she glanced back and forth from me to her boss.

"Don't worry, I won't hurt you," I said. It sounded like a line from some cheesy old action flick from the twenty-first century, the kind that only dreamed of the sort of intrigues I was now living.

"What now?" Sergei asked.

"Let's go back to your office so we can have a polite little chat," I said.

"Hmph."

"Come on," I said as I grabbed this Magdela by the arm and helped her up from the VR chair. Her skin was soft, softer than I remembered human flesh could be. She flinched at my touch, but I was firm in directing her towards the door. As Sergei led the way back to his office, I watched her follow. She wore a skin-tight black dress that came down to the knees. It was modest compared to a lot of what you saw these days—especially in her line of work—but still hugged all the right spots. She had the curves of somebody who ate well enough, but the tone of somebody who took care to stay in shape. Her dark hair hung half-way down her back despite being tied up, and it shone in the hall's lights with a healthy glimmer.

After we entered the office, I pulled the doors shut and slid a poker from a nearby fireplace through the handles to keep them closed.

Sergei went right to a sideboard bar and poured himself a glass of straight vodka, drained it, then refilled the glass. "Okay, you've got the girl. Now ask your questions and get the fuck out of my club."

I walked over to the bar. "I'd think you would want to treat a guest better than that." Finding a dusty bottle of bourbon nestled behind the vodkas, I grabbed it by the neck and brought it with me to an overstuffed armchair that sat in a circle around a small table with three mates. I plopped onto the soft chair and sighed as the aches and strains of the last two days sunk into the cushions with me.

"*Unwelcome* guest," Sergei pointed out.

"Touché."

"What is this all about?" Magdela asked as she took a seat across from me. "What questions?"

Well, down to brass tacks, then. No point trying to make small talk with a gun in my hand, anyway. I unscrewed the cap of the bourbon and took a deep swig before starting. "You know Evie Simms?"

"Of course, we work the same shift."

"You know she's dead?"

Magdela's eyes narrowed as she took a closer look at me. "Oh my God, you're Harold Jacobson! You've been all over the holovids since this morning."

I nodded. A glance at Sergei showed he was either feigning disinterest in the conversation or genuinely was more interested in whatever was underneath his fingernails than what we were saying.

"You killed Kristoff?" she asked.

Sergei's head popped up. Yep, definitely faking it. He's probably making mental notes to pass along to his mob contacts the minute I walk out the door.

"No," I said. Her eyes kept dancing from mine to the gun in my hand, so I clicked on the safety and laid it on my lap. I pulled out a cigarette and lit it up before continuing. "A Russian mobster named Boris killed Kristoff, and my partner. They're framing me for it."

Magdela's eyes shot over to Sergei before turning back to me. "Why would they kill Kristoff? He was working for them."

I wasn't sure if she was unaware this was news or unconcerned about hiding it, but she answered one of my questions without me having to ask it. I had a hunch, but the confirmation I was pulling on the right thread gave me momentum to tug harder.

"That's what I'm trying to find out, and why they killed Evie."

"Hmph." Again from Sergei, feigning disinterest despite growing more agitated by the moment. Without saying a word, he was giving me as much information as Magdela. He set down his glass with a shaking hand and leaned against his desk. "You will not find anything but an early grave. Now, can my girl get back to work?"

My eyes met Magdela's, and I saw something there pleading for me not to leave her here. Her mouth opened and closed like a goldfish spilled from its tank, and I knew there was something more she wanted to say—but couldn't.

I stood up and walked back over to the bar, put back the bourbon, and turned around. The gun was back in my hand, and I could tell Sergei hadn't missed the point since his eyes kept drifting to it. "What is it she doesn't want to tell me in front of you, Sergei?"

"I don't know what you mean. She knows nothing about Evie or Kristoff."

I took two slow, calculated steps forward. "I think she knows more than you want me to know, and I think as soon as we're out of here she's going to tell me."

Sweat beaded up on the Russian's brow and he turned to walk behind the desk. "You're grasping at phantoms, Mister Jacobson. There's nothing to connect what happened to either of them to me."

Another clue laid out without having to ask. "I didn't say they were connected to you, just that Magdela knew something about them. So, what's your part in this?" Another two steps forward brought me to the corner of the desk.

Rounding the other side, Sergei laid his hands on the polished redwood and leaned over it. "You're not going to shoot me, and I'm not going to tell you anything, so why don't you just get out?"

"Why don't you tell him about the other girls?" Magdela chimed in, either growing brave enough to speak up or afraid enough to break the tension in the room herself.

"Other girls?" I asked. This was a can of worms I had not smelled coming.

Sergei's face turned red and sweat dripped from above his ears. "Shut up, you bitch! I'll have you turning tricks in the alley if you open your whore mouth one more time!"

While his attention was on her, I stepped around the desk and slammed the handle of the pistol into the side of the Russian's head. He shrieked like a beaten stepchild as he fell to the marble tiles. Wide eyes stared back at me with a mixture of shock and fear as Sergei slithered back until his shoulders were pressed against the wall.

"What other girls?" I asked again.

Sergei pressed a hand against his head and a trickle of blood ran between his fingers. "Are you completely insane? Do you know who I am?"

I slapped him across the face with the gun, sending spit, blood, and a tooth raining down on the pristine white floor next to him. "Tell me what she knows."

"Wait!" Magdela cried out. I doubted there was any love lost between the two, but she didn't seem keen on watching me beat the man to death, either. "There were girls, a lot of them, who came to interview for jobs. Some of them left talking about getting hired, but then we never saw them again. One of them was a friend of Evie's. After she interviewed, she disappeared. Evie said her apartment was abandoned. It was like she just vanished."

"Wait..." I stepped back and leaned against the desk. "How many?"

Magdela sat back down, twisting her hands together. "I don't know, maybe two dozen over the last few weeks?"

"I'm warning you," Sergei slurred from against the wall. "Not another word."

I was tiring of his interruptions. I raised my arm, took half a second to aim, and squeezed the trigger. The smell of gunpowder and echoes of the gunshot filled the room as the bullet ripped through Sergei's thigh. I wasn't sure if it was his screams or the tinnitus from the gunshot, but a loud screeching filled my ears for several moments before fists started pounding on the office door. Voices called out from the other side.

I leveled the gun at Sergei's head. "Tell them you're okay, or you won't be giving them any more orders."

"I'm fine! Go away!" he cried out.

Magdela was slack-jawed, her eyes affixed on her boss's bleeding leg. "I can't believe..."

"He needed to be taught a lesson," I muttered as I laid the gun on the desk and lit another cigarette. "Let me get this straight. A bunch of girls went missing, and Evie knew one of them. So, she got curious and started digging. That about sum it up?"

Magdela nodded.

"Okay," I walked over to Sergei and placed a foot on his wounded leg, leaning in as I spoke, raising my voice to be heard over his cries of pain, "What was she digging into? What didn't you want her to find out?"

"It was just a business deal," Sergei groaned through gritted teeth.

"A business deal Kristoff brokered?" I asked.

Sergei laughed through tears of pain. "Really? That little shit couldn't handle his own prick without his daddy's help. He was a go-between... An errand boy."

"So why would Boris kill him?" I asked.

"The kid talked too much. Evie did some off-the-books servicing for him—unplugged servicing—and the young pup thought he was in love. He told her what was going on, and they both got silenced for their trouble."

I leaned in harder. He screamed louder. "What deal? Why has Talbot been paying you?"

Sergei caught his breath and panted out, "The girls. He pays for the girls."

It was all coming together now. Sergei was recruiting talent, and James Talbot was paying him. But was Talbot running the show, or was he just working for the mob, too? "What's the big picture?" I asked.

"I don't know. I find the girls, someone picks them up, then I get paid. That's all I know."

"Why is the Bratva involved?"

"What are they *not* involved in? You can't do business in this city without them. Come on, Jacobson, you know how this works. Now, will you get the fuck out of my club?"

I looked over at Magdela. The contempt she had for the man on the floor had grown with his admission to being party to her friend's death. I turned back to be welcomed by a smug sneer. "Yeah, we'll leave."

"We?" Magdela asked.

I flicked my cigarette onto the floor, walked back over to the bar, and grabbed the bourbon. As I headed towards the door, I waved her over. "Come on, Magdela. You can't stay here."

As I led her out of the office, Sergei called out after me, "You're a dead man, Jacobson! You'll be in hell before the sun comes up!"

"Yeah?" I called over my shoulder as I walked out. "I'll see you there."

Luckily for Magdela and me, Sergei's hired muscle weren't enthusiastic about stopping us from leaving once I flashed the steel in my hand. A few shouted curses and threats were all that assailed us as we made our way out of the club and around to the old sedan.

Magdela was shaken at first, her steps hesitant and her glance lingering over her shoulder even after the office doors were closed. But the further we got towards freedom, the more confident her steps became. By the time we were walking under the moonlight, she was practically leading the way. For her, Dreamworks probably felt like a cage—and now the lioness was free.

"What now?" she asked as we climbed into the car.

I fired up the engine and pulled out onto the road while I spoke. "First, I take you somewhere they won't come looking for you. Do you have relatives in the city? Friends?"

"I'm not hiding. They killed my best friend because of what she knew about those missing girls, and I'm going to find out why." There was a fire in her words which surprised me even after the catty walk to the car.

Firelight flashed across my face as I lit up a cigarette, and smoke curled under the brim of the old ball cap as I glanced over at her and arched an eyebrow. "You don't know what kind of trouble you're asking for. Let me take you somewhere."

She grabbed the cigarette from between my lips, took a long drag, and leaned back as the smoke coiled around stray curls of hair at her temples. Darkly shadowed eyes narrowed, and ruby-red lips pursed in condemnation. "What, you think I'm some sort of lady-child you have to take care of now? My friend is dead, and you just shot my boss in the leg. I'd say I'm fully aware of what kind of mess we're in." She took another drag from the cigarette, and I couldn't help but glance down as her chest raised and lowered with the deep breath.

I cleared my throat and pulled my attention back to the road. "Things didn't end well for my last partner, you know."

"Yeah. I saw the news, remember? Now, what's the plan?"

I sighed and dug out another cigarette as I turned the car onto the highway, headed back towards downtown. "Well, the plan had been to follow the money. I know—*we* know what the commodity being traded is now, but we still need to find out where these girls are going and who the buyer is. Talbot might be running things, or his company might just be laundering the money. Most likely, the buyer is the Bratva. But we need to connect the dots if we want to prove why Evie was murdered. I also need evidence tying Kristoff and Boris to this if I want to clear my name."

"So, we go to Talbot Construction and dig through their records?"

"Mm hmm," I mumbled. "Not sure how much help you'll be there, though."

Magdela tapped the metal implant in the back of her skull with a long, crimson fingernail shaped to a fine point. "You want to get into their computers, you need somebody who knows the inside of computers; and I doubt you have anybody who knows them like I do."

The rest of the drive downtown passed in relative silence. We were both lost in our own thoughts, brooding over our own issues. The image of Frank's face coming apart as Boris put a slug through it kept playing in my mind on a loop. I should have been trying to piece together the puzzle of how I was going to tie Kristoff into things, but thoughts of revenge consumed me.

Before I could shake them, the steel and glass towers of the business district had risen around us and I was pulling the car into an underground garage beneath the Vander Building.

The structure towered over the rest of the city, soaring a hundred stories into the night sky. Elements of Gothic architecture covered every surface which wasn't a window. Gargoyles crouched on the corners, looking out in every direction, would have been more at home on a French cathedral than an American office building. Even in the basement garage, misshapen figures of creatures from various legends adorned support columns and walls. An angel and a demon flanked the elevator doors, staring down at us as I hit the call button as if judging which of them our souls most resembled.

I didn't hesitate to escape their gaze as the elevator chimed and the doors slid open. A touchscreen on the wall offered access to the various floors of the building, but in exchange demanded security clearance in the form of biometric scans.

"I've got this," Magdela said. The fabric of her dress squeezed her hips as she crouched before the interface.

A sharp nail pulled a panel loose below it, and she set about plucking wires and swapping circuit breakers until a green light flashed on the screen. She typed in the name 'Talbot', and soon we were being whisked to the appropriate floor of the building.

I was expecting security guards, but it looked like the electronic gatekeeping was all that stood between us and our objective. I led the way through the darkened office, dim fire safety lights along the edges of the floor the only thing illuminating our path. At the end of the hall, we came to a large door with James Talbot's name on it. Again, there was a biometric security lock, but Magdela made quick work of it. She had been right; I would have been kicking in doors and probably setting off alarms if she weren't with me.

Inside, we found what one would expect from a corporate office. A modest bar sat off to one side and a seating area filled the other, resting before floor to ceiling windows looking out over the city like this was the grand tower of some king's castle. Talbot had helped build much of this city, so he probably felt like he had a right to lord over it. A massive, cherry wood desk dominated the center of the room, and the wall behind it was covered by bookshelves holding more curiosities than books. Even the latter, I suspected, were there more for gravitas than reference.

Magdela sidled around the desk and sat down in the over-sized leather chair. Her fingers flew across a glass touch display set into the desk itself, and soon a holographic monitor was beaming information back at us from a few inches above it. She sailed through menus faster than I could read them and bypassed security checks as if she were solving a set of children's riddles.

"Anything?" I asked, impatient despite her swift progress.

"Just about... Aha!" She placed her fingers around a square of information and pulled them apart, bringing it up larger than life floating over the desk. "Here, it looks like whenever Talbot sent money to Sergei, there was a specific ship scheduled to depart with less than a day's notice: the *Beverly*. Looks like a freighter. And on the surface, it's running manufactured steel construction components to a buyer in Vladivostok."

Things just got even more troubling. Were they shipping these girls overseas? I was worried they were getting buried in some local cyber dens where they'd be jacked in full-time and kept under with a cocktail of drugs and intravenous nutrients. But if they were sending them to Russia, it would be almost impossible to track them down. I rubbed the stubble on my face with a calloused hand. I was a glorified beat cop, not some kind of international spy. I was in way over my head, and the more I tried to reach the surface, the deeper the abyss grew.

"Why do you look like I just stepped on your puppy's neck?" Magdela asked as she rummaged around the desk drawers. She found what she had been looking for, a data chip, and slid it into a slot on the desk. "With this, we can tie Talbot to Dreamworks. We just take this to the police, and you're in the clear."

"Not that easy, sweetheart," I muttered as I lit up a smoke and plopped onto the couch. "That's all circumstantial. He could have been paying Sergei for anything, and the timing of the shipments could be a coincidence. And this still doesn't help us fit Kristoff into the puzzle."

"Oh, but this does," Magdela said as she pulled up another file. "Looks like Kristoff was getting paid at the same time as Sergei. Maybe a founder's fee? He had been bragging about helping to recruit the girls for Sergei."

"It's a step in the right direction, but it's still a bunch of scattered pieces with nothing to glue them together. Your statement as a witness is really the only connecting factor, and that will not convince the D.A. there's a criminal conspiracy going on."

"Well," Magdela said as she pulled the data chip from the desk and made it disappear below the neckline of her dress. "The *Beverly* is in port right now, and the most recent payment to Sergei was made today. I guess we'll have to go to the docks and see what's on this ship."

*   *   *

The drive to the docks brought us back through The Dale, but it was over in minutes by car; a stark contrast to spending nearly a day on foot to get through there yesterday. The docks themselves weren't anything to write home about: warehouses, cranes, stacks of shipping containers, and wharves with an assortment of large and small craft moored. For all the innovation which went into rebuilding New Angeles after the big quake hit, the docks looked like they might have in the past. The only difference was the harbor now sat where old downtown Los Angeles used to be, and out there beneath the waves Santa Monica and Long Beach were now the two largest man-made reefs on the west coast.

I switched the lights of the car off and drifted between the metal warehouses and shipping containers. Magdela and I both craned our necks looking for any sign of trouble, but the harbor seemed to be as deserted as one would expect it to be at two in the morning. Rain was patting down; the gentle drops might have lulled a younger me to sleep, but now only echoed my malaise.

"We're looking for bay sixty-five," Magdela said as we drew close to the main dockyard. Looming behemoths rocked in their berths as the breeze picked up and the still waters of the harbor churned under the weight of an oncoming storm.

We turned a corner and knew we had found our quarry. Ahead was a flurry of activity as cranes loaded rows of the hollow steel bricks onto the deck of a freighter. Flood lights illuminated a scene of organized chaos as workers ran back and forth, readying the next load for its short flight. Several cars and trucks were parked in a row facing the ship, their headlights all adding to the illumination of the mid-night loading party.

The wet brakes of the old car squeaked slightly as I brought it to a stop behind a stack of coiled crane cables. I winced and waited for the shouts of alarm from the clandestine gathering ahead, but the slight noise must have been lost in the night. I looked at Magdela and said, "Stay here."

She shook her head, those few loose curls around her temples bobbing as if they were also disagreeing with me. "No, you might need me. Let's go." Without another word, she was out of the car and drifting through the shadows.

Despite the high heels and a dress more suited to a cocktail party than espionage, she danced from shadow to shadow with impressive ease. I followed behind clumsily, realizing if they caught us, it would more than likely be my fault. We made our way to the rows of cargo containers being readied for loading and took shelter in the shadows behind them.

Magdela pulled a phone out—where she had been keeping it was beyond me—and started taking pics of the gathered workers. Somebody called out a few words in Russian, and one of the SUVs parked alongside the wharf opened and disgorged its contents. Five women, all young and beautiful, were led towards the containers. Their faces were bruised, clothes torn, and any makeup had long since run down their cheeks in rivers of tears. I made sure Magdela was getting images of them, then held a hand out for her to stay put and crept around the side of the container.

Workers pulled the front open as some goons in suits led the girls towards it. They were all armed, some of them with military grade assault rifles. I peered through the growing haze as the rain fell even harder. Thunder crashed in the distance and a flash of lightning illuminated the face of one of the men: Boris.

My heart pounded as the image of Frank's face coming apart again flooded my mind. Boris's ugly mug was right next to mine, his breath hot on my neck as he held the gun in my hand and squeezed my finger over the trigger.

Before I knew what I was doing, cold steel was in my hand once again. I jumped out from my hiding spot with the pistol in my hand and screamed, "Boris!"

Then all hell broke loose.

I don't know what I had expected to happen in that moment. Maybe something out of an action hero movie, where the underdog cop and his criminal nemesis faced off in single combat while all the goons stood there and watched. Instead, Boris yelled orders in Russian and a dozen goons opened fire. I ducked back around the corner of the container as bullets ricocheted from it and the damp concrete beneath my feet. Magdela screamed something at me, but it was lost in the chaos of the moment.

I ran to her, grabbed her by the arm, and made a beeline towards the crane cables hiding our car.

"You're an idiot!"

I heard her that time. I couldn't disagree with her, either. The fervent desire for revenge had boiled over and taken place of any rational thought for just a moment, and that moment had been all it took to turn our little spy game upside down.

We were almost there. A few more yards and we'd be ducking around the spools and climbing into the car. I looked back over my shoulder. Several men were giving chase, but most of them were content to either shoot from a distance or stay out of the way. The girls were gone, probably herded into one of those cargo boxes. *How many of them were already loaded? How many more were waiting?*

Concern for the kidnapped girls quickly faded from my mind as a sharp pain tore through my side. I called out in agony as I spun and fell, splashing through growing puddles into the shadow of a warehouse. Magdela kneeled over me, grabbing my shoulders. Rough concrete scraped over my thighs as she dragged me deeper into the night. Gunfire and shouts faded as steel slammed on steel and a monster growled in my ears. The world rumbled, and the odor of blood filled my nose. Something squealed and I could tell we were moving. Then a sudden stop, and acceleration in the other direction. Lights flashed overhead, filtered into a rainbow of colors through rainwater beading on glass.

Magdela looked back at me, her face a mask of worry. I locked in on those ruby red lips and almond-shaped eyes as darkness crept into the edges of my vision, slowly closing me off from her.

"You're an idiot."

I had heard those words before, not long ago. They had been shouted in anger then, but this time they seemed to carry a weight of concern—maybe even compassion.

Strong light glowed against my eyelids, and I cracked them open. Pain seared through my head as the light hit my eyes, and I squeezed them shut. A groan escaped my lips as I tried to roll over, but a firm hand on my shoulder held me down.

"Lie still."

The voice was soothing, and I relented as fresh waves of torment rippled through my body. It felt like a rod of hot iron was being pressed through my abdomen. I took a few deep breaths and surrendered to the soft surface below me.

Was it a bed?

Everything hurt, but the softness below me felt like heaven. Smooth fabrics slid across my skin. My shirt was gone. I could feel bruises on my shoulders and hips where Magdela had dragged me across the docks. Memories drifted through my mind, but they were fleeting and unsure. Cargo containers, rain, yelling, and gunshots. That all seemed familiar. Everything now seemed wrong. The bright light, the soft bed, the smooth skin of gentle hands against my bare shoulder.

Strange smells filled my nostrils. Flowers, fruit, and... bacon? I heard metal and porcelain clanking nearby, all undercut by the soft sizzle of fat rendering.

"Is he awake?" Another voice, this one sounding far away, carried to my ears. It was a woman. Thoughts of my ex-wife drifted through my mind. *Are you awake*? she would call from the kitchen in the wee hours of the morning. Those odd smells suddenly became more familiar. Potpourri, perfume, and cleaning chemicals masked with the scent of flowers and citrus. I hadn't lived with a woman in almost ten years, but the familiarity of the scene came rushing back. I wasn't sure if I should feel relieved or terrified, considering what it had been like last time I was in such a place.

"Yeah, kind of." The first voice, nearby. So close I could feel the words as much as hear them.

Magdela.

I opened my eyes again, this time slowly and with a hand shading them from the harsh light overhead. Magdela sat next to me, on the edge of a bed covered in a flowery duvet. Her hair was plastered around her face, dark curls framing pale skin. There was a flush in her cheeks of genuine concern rather than the painted-on variety. Most of her makeup had washed off in the rain, but she was still beautiful, sitting over me like some guardian angel.

Pastel rose walls surrounded us. Curtains speckled with butterflies covered a window, illuminated by the occasional flash of lightning from outside. Porcelain dolls sat along one wall, a silent audience to this strange melodrama. Thunder rumbled through the room as my pulse pounded in my temples.

"Where?" I asked.

"We're at a friend's apartment," Magdela said as she brushed some stray hair from my forehead. Lightning seems to surge through me as her fingers brushed against my skin. Her touch was soft and gentle. She cocked her head to one side and smiled, those ruby lips parting to reveal pearl-white teeth. Her eye shadow was smudged, and mascara was smeared across her cheeks. She hadn't even taken the time to wash up. She had probably been sitting there watching over me, but...

"How long?" I groaned and tried to sit up again, but those soft hands turned firm as she pushed down on my shoulders. Something about the simple act stirred something inside me; a heat of passion I hadn't felt in years. I wanted to fight back, to get to my feet and get back on the case. But even more, I wanted her to stop me.

"Lie still. You've only been out for about an hour. We're in downtown, at my friend Alice's apartment. She helped me patch you up."

"What happened?" I groaned. I remembered rain and lightning. The ship and the girls. And...

"Boris!" I almost shot out of the bed, but again she held me down.

"They shot you. It went right through. You're lucky Alice is a nurse; she was able to fix you up. But you have to rest now." She grabbed a cold rag from a bedside table and wiped the beads of sweat I hadn't even realized were on my forehead. Pain shot through my side again, and I surrendered back into the soft mattress below me.

As I lay there, the fog parted and my memories coalesced. The docks. The girls being loaded into cargo containers. The mobsters, and Boris. I fought to sit up again and almost screamed out as another wave of pain seared my abdomen. I placed a hand on my belly and felt gauze and medical tape covering it.

"I told you to stop," Magdela said more forcibly this time, leaning over me to push me back into the bed. Her hands wrapped around my wrists and her face blocked the light. My eyes finally focused, and all I could see were those ruby lips. Magdela's hair, still wet from the rain, cascaded around my face. Her chest pressed against mine, her bosom peeking out from under her little black dress and soft against my bare chest.

"Do I have to climb on top of you to get you to lie still?" she asked. Her breath was hot on my neck. Faded perfume mixed with stale rainwater and the sweat of the night's business filled my nose.

"Only if you want to," I whispered.

Her lips met mine.

Almost dying together could spark something in two total strangers. Humankind had a passion for life, and nothing stoked those fires like the threat of death. Our lips pressed together with a primal urge, and she parted hers slightly to let my tongue inside her. Hands groped roughly across flesh, and the pain from the gunshot faded as a new throbbing took precedence in my mind.

"Hey guys, breakfast is rea—" Alice stopped herself in the doorway. "Oh, for fuck's sake. Breakfast for one, as always," she sighed as she pulled the door closed.

* * *

The first orange glow of dawn was just coloring the clouds in the east as I stood before the window, looking out over the city. Steel and concrete stretched almost as far as I could see, and beyond that, great mountains rose like a wall around the mass of humanity. Past those mountains was the desert, and as far as I'd ever been.

"What's out there?" Magdela asked from under the blankets.

"I don't know," I answered. Maybe it was a better life, or more likely just more of the same. New Angeles wasn't an island of decadence. All across the country, and even the world, the urban sprawl had taken over. Suburbs had given way to slums as the middle class ceased to exist long ago. The countryside was a lawless badland where the only sign of order were the massive corporate farms guarded by private armies. The American dream had been a lie, and now all that mattered was survival, or the next drink, or the next score.

I turned away from the horizon and all the hopelessness it represented, and looked back at Magdela as she got dressed. She wasn't the most attractive woman I'd run into lately, or the funniest. She was probably the strongest, though. There was a fire in the woman which refused to be quenched—a drive to put things right. That kind of hope, that kind of passion, was rare these days. Because of this, Magdela was one of a kind.

"Hungry?" she asked.

I nodded, also realizing I hadn't had a cigarette since I'd woken up in the apartment. "Can we smoke in here?"

"I think Alice can make an exception, considering you've been shot."

I pulled my shirt on, wincing as the newly stitched wound on my side protested. I tucked the gun into my waistband out of habit and followed Magdela out to the main room of the apartment. This space didn't scream femininity as much as the bedroom, but it still felt fancy compared to what I was used to. Oak shelves dotted the walls, filled with ceramic statues of fanciful creatures like dragons and unicorns. Framed paintings filled the empty spaces, sporting castles and meadows. Books were strewn about everywhere, like Alice was reading them all at once and no matter where she went, one was within reach.

Speaking of our host, she was sitting on the couch with a book in her hand. Her blond hair was pulled back into a tight ponytail and thick glasses covered her eyes. With an apartment like this, she should be able to afford ocular implants, but she still used the archaic old external lenses. In fact, everything about this woman screamed old-fashioned. The books, the fantasy art, the glasses... it all seemed like a relic from a hundred years ago. *Was she holding out hope things could be this way, or was she just escaping to a better place?* Probably the latter.

"Alice, do you have an ashtray?" Magdela asked as she rummaged around in the kitchen.

"No, I don't smoke," Alice said, peering out over the top of the book at me. Her eyes betrayed the embarrassed grin she was hiding behind the pages. Probably not every day Alice's friend brings a random guy to her apartment, bleeding from a gunshot wound, then has sex with him in her bed.

"It's fine." Magdela walked out into the sitting area with a small steel saucepan holding an inch of water. "This'll do."

I sat down in a cushy armchair and lit up a smoke.

Magdela sat on the couch next to Alice and did the same before asking, "So, what's our next move?"

"I'm not sure. We're out of strings to pull." I took a drag of the cigarette and tapped the ash into the saucepan.

"Then we take what we have and go to the police. We connected Dreamworks to Talbot, and him to the mob. We have pictures of the girls at the docks. If we hurry, they might even stop the ship from leaving the harbor," Magdela said.

I shook my head. "No, it won't happen that fast. We probably have a good enough case for the courts, but Talbot will fight it. With the kind of money he has, he'll have the best lawyers, too. Hell, he might have every judge in town in his pocket. Even if he gets convicted, it'll take years to duke it out in the system. Meanwhile, they've made public enemy number one out of me on the holovids. As soon as we walk in the door, they'll lock me up, and fallen cops don't last a week on the inside. I'll probably get shivved on the first day. And you," I paused to take another drag of the cigarette, "are going to be hunted down by every goon in the city. You have to leave... *today*."

"No," Magdela said. "Everybody I know is here. I can't just leave."

"Don't be stupid," Alice said. "Why don't you both just leave town? Go start over together out east?"

It was a good question. I doubt I'd made national news. With the new barcode, I could go east and start a new life. Maybe settle down as a private dick in New York. I could leave all this behind and start over. Walk away from it all and never look back. My eyes met Magdela's, and I could see she was thinking the same thing. There was a sorrow there. The light of passion was being eclipsed by the memory of her friend's murder and the fate of all those girls being shipped overseas, probably to be sold off as sex slaves or to be crammed into a Russian cyber den. I could tell

Magdela was just waiting for me to cut and run, snuffing out her spark of hope once and for all.

I rubbed a hand across my face. "No. What's happening here isn't right, and I couldn't live with myself if I just walked away from it. Somebody has to do something, and right now we're the only ones who can bring this to light."

Magdela sighed and shot me a smile which threatened to thaw what little ice was left in my veins. Was I going soft? Was it her fault, or was this about revenge for Frank, a partner I couldn't stand in life and can't forget about in death? Either way, here I was, and I had to figure out what to do next.

"So," Alice cut in, "get this Talbot guy to confess."

It sounded ridiculous, but the more I thought about it, the more sense it made. Were this still a typical police investigation, I'd have enough evidence to confront the primary suspect. I'd haul him to HQ and lock him in a room to be grilled until he spilled the beans. Of course, Talbot was one of the untouchables. I could never haul a man with that kind of money and power in like some street punk. But this wasn't a police investigation. This was something else now, and the rules weren't the same.

"That's just crazy enough to work," I muttered.

"I don't see any other options," Magdela said. "Let's go."

"No," I said as I dropped the butt in the shallow pot of water. "This is still too dangerous. You stay here where you'll be safe."

"Oh, hell no," she said as she rose and opened a box on a bookshelf. She pulled a small pistol from it, slapped a magazine home, and yanked back on the slide. "I've gotten you this far, and I'm not letting you finish it alone."

The rising sun infused the smog-covered city with an orange glow by the time we drove up to the Vander Building. Those gargoyles stared down at us from every corner, even the entrance to the underground parking garage, as if trying to warn us off from this course of action. Inside the garage, spaces were filling up as the drones arrived for the daily grind. The old sedan sputtered as we drifted between pedestrians. The rusty old car was as out of place here as we were. It didn't belong, and its presence was disturbing the order of things.

I pulled it into an open space between two sports cars, which probably never reached their full potential on the congested city streets. Magdela and I got out and headed towards the elevator along with the throng, trying our best to blend in. My pistol nagged at the small of my back as I walked, reminding me there was a good chance things would end badly here. Magdela fidgeted with the holster strapped to her thigh under her dress, probably feeling the same unease from trying to blend into the crowd while packing heat.

We passed between the demon and the angel flanking the elevator. I still wasn't sure which I was more akin to. I never considered myself a hero. Hell, I never even considered myself a good cop. I just did my job and collected my paycheck. Now here I was on some crusade of justice—or vengeance. Which it was still wasn't clear.

The security panel in the elevator hadn't been fixed, and the occupants all muttered with curiosity lacking genuine concern as they punched in their destinations. Magdela reached out and tapped the floor for Talbot's office, remembering which it was from the night before. The ride up seemed to take forever, stopping every several floors to disgorge more passengers. The number of people in the car fell as we rose, until finally it was just the two of us riding to the very top of the building. There was a soft, inviting chime, then the doors slid open and the final few steps of this crazy night were before us.

Motes of dust danced in horizontal rays of sunlight as the morning light shot through the windows on the east side of the building. The offices on our right were backlit by the sunrise, while those on our left were bathed in shadow. It was still too early for the executives who populated this floor to be here yet, but gruff shouting from the end of the hall revealed one early bird was already biting the head off some worm.

We ambled down the hallway between the rows of empty offices. At the end of it was the door with James Talbot's name on it, and behind it the yelling continued. I reached out, pushed the door open, and we stepped inside.

A burly man—barrel-chested and almost as broad at the shoulder as he was tall—paced behind the desk screaming into a phone. "I don't want to hear any excuses, just make it happen." Spittle flew out of his mouth and coated the clear glass. Then he stabbed at it with his thumb to hang up and dropped the phone on the desk with a loud rattle. He stood there staring at us for a moment, seeming to size us up. "Well, you must be the two who caused all the commotion last night. Harold, is it? And..."

"Nobody," I said before Magdela could answer. If he didn't know her name, it was best to keep it that way.

"No matter," Talbot said as he grabbed a half-smoked, smoldering cigar from a crystal ashtray and clenched it between his teeth. He sat in the chair behind the desk and leaned back, as casual as if this were just another day in the office for him. "So, I can assume you're the one who shot Sergei?"

"You can assume all you want," I said as I sat in a chair in front of the desk. I pulled out a cigarette and lit it up, trying to mask my apprehension and match Talbot's demeanor. He slid the ashtray across the desk, making a loud scraping noise in the uncomfortable silence.

He puffed at the cigar; his eyes locked on mine. "I want you to know you've caused me an inconvenience, and I don't let slights like that go unanswered. You're already the most wanted man in the city. Why not just disappear?"

Magdela pulled out her phone and handed it to me. I pulled up an image of the girls being herded into the shipping containers and slid it across the desk. "That's why."

Talbot glanced at the screen for a moment, then slid the phone back with a dismissive shove. "So what? Some cunts down at the docks. What's this got to do with me?"

"They were being loaded onto the *Beverly*, one of your freighters. We also have the records of payments from the Russians to you, and you to Dreamworks, all coinciding with this and other shipments."

"Oh, I see," Talbot nodded and stood. He paced over to the window and looked out over the city, still puffing away at the broad cigar. "So, you think you have it all figured out, and now I'm suddenly going to cave and admit to the whole thing. You think I'm going to clear you of all wrong, admit my own business associates killed my nephew and framed you for it, and then you're going to go back to work."

"That's about it," Magdela said. "You piece of shit. You think you can just buy and sell people? You think you can just get rid of them when they get in your way? That's not how things work."

"That's *exactly* how things work!" Talbot yelled as he spun away from the window. A red flush rose in his cheeks and a single vein throbbed in his forehead. Smoke wreathed him from the cigar in his hand as he gesticulated to punctuate his words. "You think you can come into my office and intimidate me? You think you can change anything about what's happening in my city? I practically built this city. It's *mine*. And the cattle inside it are mine to do with as I please."

"You're a monster!" Magdela yelled, rising to her feet as well. "Those are people. She was my *friend.*"

Talbot stopped and met her eyes, realization dawning behind his own. "Is she what this is all about? That little bitch from the flesh bar? If she had been a good little girl and just done her job, she'd still be alive. She asked too many questions, and she got what she had coming to her for it."

Magdela was about to say something else, but I stood up and laid a hand on her shoulder. Tears streamed down her face. I took a step in front of her and said, "You may think that's how things work, but there are laws, Mister Talbot. Society can't operate without them, and nobody is above them."

"Oh?" Talbot arched an eyebrow. "And what are you, some holy crusader of justice? I read your file, Mister Jacobson. I know all about you. Your rap sheet is as long as any of the scumbags you put away. Police brutality, taking bribes, abusing narcotics..."

"Nobody's perfect," I muttered. Having my own record thrown in my face put me off pace.

"Oh? And what about that ex-wife of yours? What about putting her in the hospital missing half her teeth? I'd say that's quite *far* from perfect, Mister Jacobson."

Magdela's head jerked around, her eyes meeting mine with a mix of confusion and disgust.

"Oh, so the new strumpet doesn't know you're a wife beater?" Talbot grinned and took another puff of his cigar. "I guess that's not something you share on the first date, is it?"

"This isn't about me," I growled. I could feel a wave of warmth rising through my scalp. Was it anger or embarrassment? I'd kept that particular skeleton locked in my closet for ten years. I wasn't prepared to have it dragged out and paraded before me. Not here. Not now.

"Oh, but isn't it? You're spouting on about laws. Your little bitch is screeching about how 'things don't work this way'. But you're sitting there on your white horses like a couple of righteous angels while trudging knee-deep in your own shit."

Talbot walked back over to the desk and picked up the phone with the image of the girls at the docks still displayed on it. "*This* is how the world works. And people like me are the ones calling the shots. You don't get to prance in here and demand otherwise. You're just a couple of nobodies, and that's all you'll ever be." He took another puff on the cigar and put the phone back on the desk. "Well, maybe except for you, Harold. You're a famous cop killer. At least you'll be remembered for *something*."

"You're wrong," Magdela said with a forced calm as she picked up the phone. "Now we have your confession. I've been recording you this whole time. Give it up, Talbot. We got you."

Laughter roared through the office and Talbot's face turned an even deeper shade of red as a sudden coughing fit overcame him. He bent over double, his hand holding him up by the corner of the desk. "Oh, that's almost as rich as I am." He caught his breath, stood up straight, and walked back over to the window.

"What's so funny?" I asked.

Talbot gestured out at the city lying below us. The sun had risen above the mountains, and shadows cast by the city's towers stretched towards the Vander Building like the arms of beggars reaching out for alms from the icon of wealth lording over them. "You really think any of this matters? You think I can't bury your so-called evidence, and you along with it? I told you, *I own this city*." Spittle flew out of Talbot's mouth as he shouted the last. "Every cop, every lawyer, and every judge belong to me. Hell, my fucking sister is the mayor. Do you really think this will get past the district attorney's desk? I'm his daughter's godfather, for Christ's sake. I paid her way through college. Go ahead, file your report. You'll be rotting in prison for killing Kristoff and all of your evidence will be destroyed before they even lock the cell."

Magdela slumped into a chair, defeated. The spark of hope I saw in her eyes just a few hours ago was extinguished, and all that was left was the deep pit of hopelessness which could be seen in every other pair of eyes in the city.

Something inside of me snapped in the moment. Seeing her light snuffed out tore away the only glimmer of hope I'd seen in over a decade. She looked at me like I was a monster after learning of my past, which eroded any thoughts of happiness returning to my life. There was nothing left then but anger. Anger over Frank's death. Anger at being framed for it and

Kristoff's murder. Anger about all those women being taken and shipped off to a life of servitude.

And most of all, anger that Talbot was right. I was angry this *was* how things worked, and there wasn't anything anybody could do about it.

Talbot must have seen that hope die inside me, because he strode over and poked a finger into my chest. "You see it now, don't you Harold? You see how stupid you've been, chasing some dream of justice in a world where it doesn't exist. There's only one true law in the world, and there only ever has been one law. The powerful rule over the weak. The Romans knew it, the British knew it, and now you see the light."

He walked back over to the window with his back to us. "Once, it was the might of steel that ruled the land. Now, it's the almighty dollar. Whoever controls the money, controls the world. You've known this for a long time, Harold, you just didn't want to admit it. What have you ever done in life which wasn't fueled by greed? You didn't become a cop because of some sense of justice. You did it because it paid a decent wage and had good benefits. Hell, you even beat your wife half to death over money, didn't you?" He spun on me, a sardonic grin crossing his face. "What was it? Was she buying too many shoes? Spending it all on fancy jewelry? There was enough, though, wasn't there? You could afford it; you just wanted more for yourself. There were things you wanted—booze, drugs, whatever—but that bitch was spending all your money." He turned around again and took a puff of the cigar. "We're a lot like each other, Harold. That's the tragedy in all this. You might have been somebody if you hadn't been on the wrong side and start this little war of yours."

I looked back at Magdela, who still slumped over in the chair. She met my gaze, but what I saw there surprised me. There was a wondering, as if she were considering Talbot might be right about me. But there was also a desire to hear me defend myself. She still wanted to believe there was some good in the world, despite Talbot shattering any idea of it over and over again.

I wanted to tell her there was something pure about me, that Talbot was wrong, but I couldn't. I knew there had to be some good in the world, but she wouldn't find it with me. I was as much of a rotten bastard as

Talbot was making me out to be, and I had no defense for it.

The little good I'd hoped to find in the world had rested with Magdela, and if she was looking to me for that spark of hope, then we were all truly lost.

"So, go ahead," Talbot interrupted my thoughts. "Take your evidence to the police. Turn yourself in. I'll be here. While you're rotting in prison, I'll be here building my own Pax Romana. This city needs me, after all. I'm the only thing holding it together. Without me, it would all crumble into chaos. There has to be a wolf to tend the flock, else the sheep will tear themselves apart."

I looked out over his shoulder at the city as the sun rose above it, and beyond to the mountains. Great swaths of desert stretched out beyond them, and past that the promise of a new life. I could still walk away from all this. Away from Talbot. Away from New Angeles. I could run away from my past and start a new life. I looked back, and Magdela's eyes still searched my own for some glimmer of hope in a world full of darkness.

I turned back and fixed my gaze squarely on Talbot's back. He took another puff of his cigar as he looked out over *his* city. I should just let him have it. I shouldn't try to change what can't be changed. Still, the way things were wasn't the way they had to be. Something in my mind screamed for me to change all of this.

"You're wrong about one thing, Mister Talbot," I said as I pulled the pistol from behind my back.

He turned, his grin of contempt still on his face. It slid away as he recognized the glint of steel in my hand. The smile faded, to be replaced by a twisted mask of confusion. Even in this moment, he couldn't accept the idea of somebody rallying against what he saw to be the natural order of things.

My finger slid over the trigger as I leveled the gun. My hand should have been shaking, but it was as steady as my newfound conviction. I squeezed softly and the silence in the room was broken as the hammer struck down on the primer. The pistol roared as flame and smoke flashed from the barrel. A single round flew out, spinning with the frenzy of the downtrodden masses who simply could not take this anymore. The lead slug drilled into the flesh of Talbot's forehead, shattered bone, and tore through his brain. Bits of flesh and skull erupted behind him, and blood splattered against the window a moment before the slug continued its journey and shattered the glass. Talbot fell back through the spinning shards as the morning sun reflected off them in a sparkling shower of light. A broken man fell from his ivory tower, limp and helpless as the bits of broken glass falling around him.

I looked out over the precipice and whispered, "There are wolves among the sheep."

The bell over the door rang out to herald my entrance as I walked into Rosie's Diner in Sanrita. The usual evening crowd was there: tired office drones slumped over tepid coffee, gangbangers with an eye for a fresh mark, and pushers taking time from their busy routine to satiate the base need of sustenance.

Rosie cocked her head to the side as I walked up to the counter, an eye still twitching from faulty wiring. The damaged hand from her run-in with the local street toughs was wrapped in duct tape, covering the singed wiring beneath.

I sat down at the counter and scanned my wrist over the barcode reader set into it. Rosie blinked as the diner's network sent my payment information directly to her robotic brain. She looked at me, smiled, and winked with her twitchy eye as she said, "Nice to see you again, *Jasper*. What'll it be?"

"Two coffees," I said as I took the fedora off my head and set it on the counter. I pulled my cigarettes out of the long trench coat pocket and lit one. The smoke felt good going down, the coarse warmth burning my throat and reminding me for one more moment that I was still alive.

The door chimed again.

"Two?" Rosie asked.

"You heard the man," Magdela said as she sidled up to the counter and took the stool next to me. She took the cigarette from my fingers and placed it between her ruby lips. The cherry lit up her face in the dim lighting of the diner as she drew on it, and smoke framed the curls at her temples. Her black outfit contrasted with her ivory skin, making it seem as if it were glowing. The leather jacket's high collar helped hide the implant in the back of her skull, but the tight pants did little to hide the curves of her hips.

Rosie smiled in a way that was both genuine and artificial, the way only a sentient machine could. "Two coffees, coming right up."

I took the steaming cup and nodded my thanks. The robot moved on along the counter, and I turned around to survey the crowd. The coffee went down hot and scalding, black and strong. Again, a little reminder that I was still alive. I recognized a lot of the faces in the diner. Stitch and Razor, two local gangbangers who were almost always found in the booth by the front door, were there as usual. They were the two which had fucked up Rosie's hand a few weeks ago, but she had insisted I not get involved. They were enforcers for a local outfit called the Chimeras who claimed this area as their territory, and Rosie had to pay into their protection racket. I could bump the two off, but more would come to replace them. No... I had bigger fish to fry.

"So," Magdela said at my elbow. "What's on the agenda for tonight?"

I took another sip of coffee and turned towards her. "Recruiting," I said, then stood and walked towards the door. She downed the rest of her java and followed me.

I stopped beside the booth where Stitch and Razor sat. Leather and shining steel spikes covered them. The backs of their jackets had the image of their gang's namesake, a mythological creature blending the features of a lion, goat, and serpent in bright green, purple, and blue. Brightly colored hair stood up in fans and spikes over the shaved sides of their heads. Steel chains adorned their necks and wrists. Stitch looked up at me and grinned. "You've got a lot of nerve showing your face in public, detective."

"It's not detective anymore. Just Jasper," I said as I lit another cigarette to replace the one Magdela took.

"Nice name, where'd you buy it?" Razor asked, laughing at what he thought was a clever jab at my expense.

"The Glen."

The two looked at each other and nodded in approval, surprise washing over their faces as they realized I wasn't on the other side of the law from them anymore. "Okay," Stitch said, "what do you want?"

"Come with me," I said. "I've got a job for you two."

Fog rolled through the alleys of New Angeles as the four of us padded into the night. Neon light cut through the mist, the constant buzzing of the chemical signs seeming to hum a melody accompanied by the steady rhythm of rain falling on the city. No matter how much rain fell, the filth would not wash from those streets.

But if enough people stand up and say they won't take it anymore—if the sheep shed their wool and reveal the wolves within—perhaps things will change.

About the Author

B.K. Bass is the author of over a dozen works of science fiction, fantasy, and horror inspired by the pulp fiction magazines of the early 20th century and classic speculative fiction. He is a student of history with a particular focus on the ancient, classical, and medieval eras. B.K. has a lifetime of experience with a specialization in business management and human relations and served in the U.S. Army as a Nuclear, Chemical, and Biological Operations Specialist. When B.K. isn't dreaming up new worlds to explore, he spends his time as a bookworm, film buff, and strategy gamer.

Find out more and connect with B.K. at https://bkbass.com

Harold's story concludes in **NIGHT SHADOW!**

New Angeles is in turmoil. The government, the corporations, and the mob have New Angeles in an iron grip that continues to tighten. But, the people have decided they will not take it anymore. As the city burns and all-out rebellion is sparked, Harold must finally decide where his loyalties lay.

Discover more exciting adventures at

BKBASS.COM

www.ingramcontent.com/pod-product-compliance
Ingram Content Group UK Ltd.
Pitfield, Milton Keynes, MK11 3LW, UK
UKHW040010200726
13854UKWH00001B/126

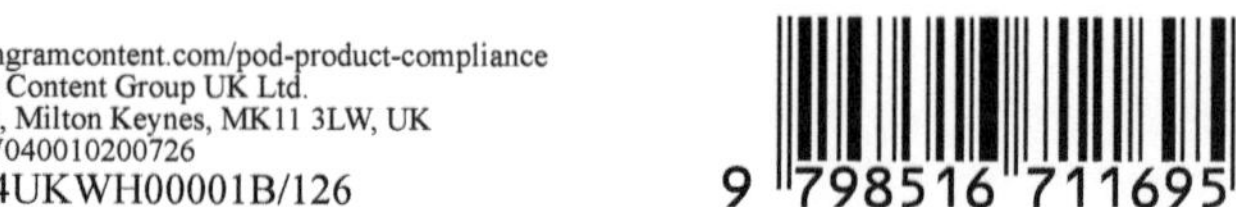